The Dream House

Laura Dockrill

illustrated by Gwen Millward

Piccadilly
P R E S S

For Krissy Wardie – thank you for the dreams x

For Max love GM (mum) x

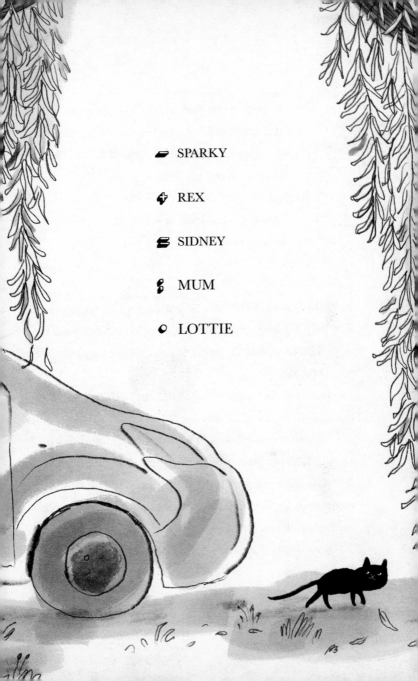

1.

The scrampled ground is thick with stones. I meet a stag beetle on the way in, alone on the ground in a makeshift graveyard of pebbles, and say *hello* but it's dead.

➤ *It's dead.*

my godfather says. Which is weird in itself as we don't really believe in God.

2.

I like the sound of the wheels of my suitcase on the tiles. Rattling. Chalky and wobbling and loose under each step. The pieces all slipping out like pieces in a jigsaw.

Typical.

Just like the ground beneath me. Always falling through these days.

I know the smell well. The smell of antique shops. Damp. Like old postcards or museums. Like books from the past with cracked browning spines and not much room between the lines, with pages that make your eyes turn blind if you look too long.

Sometimes I look too long and I won't even know I'm doing it.

3.

The last time I heard Sparky's voice I didn't see him. It was back *then*. At our house. I had my back against my bedroom door.

🖝 *Rex . . . can I come in?*

I didn't answer because I've learned not to trust those soft voices too much. They lure you in as if it's about a simple surface thing, but really it's to try to get something bigger out of you. Soft voices do that; they smoke you out.

But I didn't push the door as hard as I could. If he'd pushed harder, he would have been able to get in.

But he gave up.

4.

There were too many people downstairs in the house that day. Lottie was behaving like it was a birthday party, wanting to show everybody her bedroom and her toys. She'd been given so many toys since everything; it had made her a bit 'expecting'. She kind of thought that's what people did all the time to everybody, even when it wasn't even a present-giving time. That's because people didn't know how to help, how to be, how to say sorry, so they'd overcompensate with gifts. But they weren't helping. They were just transforming Lottie into a greedy spoilt monster.

And Lottie didn't know him like I did. I just wanted everybody to leave.

Mum changed her outfit five times that day and kept wiping her eyes the whole time. That's crying without letting yourself cry. It's worse than actual crying because everybody knows that's what it is but nobody can say, 'Are you all right?'

At one point she sang that song 'Don't You (Forget About Me)' into a French baguette. People didn't know whether to clap and laugh or cry.

Eventually they went home after they'd eaten all the good crisps and used up all the toilet roll.

Good riddance.

5.

The van journey was silent except for Sparky's humming.
Which was OK.

But now we are here, with the yellow door with the
cracked paint. The spy hole. The ghost of me as a child.

➤ *That's all you in there . . .*

Sparky says, pointing at the drawers. He keeps a
camera, my godfather. He takes pictures of everything

and the hallway is an antique filing cabinet
stuffed with our faces: too much chocolate
cake and rollercoaster rides and piggybacks
on the beach.

There'll be lots of *him* in there too but I
don't want to look at those today.

Or maybe even ever.

6.

The wallpaper is creamy and dark red and covered in gold pointy stars. And there are little glass boxes with all weird stuff in them like pinned butterflies and a white mouse frozen in the position it had died. Its death looks sudden. An expression of shock. Fear. Panic. *Even* on the face of a mouse.

That is probably why Sparky is a vegetarian – because he knows the look of terror on the face of a mouse.

I wonder why the butterflies made it into a piece of art but the stag beetle wasn't special enough to even make it inside the front door.

7.

The kitchen is all cluttered wooden cupboards and always, as I remember, a big brown loaf on a chopping board and a massive jar of Marmite. That's what you live on if you're vegetarian: Marmite on toast.

Oh, and broccoli. You can eat broccoli too. As much as you like, in fact.

8.

My room is made up. Simple and small. A single bed and a wardrobe filled with a jumble of metal hangers all tangled together like an oversized bunch of keys.

Sparky and I haven't spent time together on our own for a while. But I know he's kept an eye on me through the big mad eye of his nosy camera lens, capturing me when he could. Watching me from afar. Secretly I am glad he was always there, like some CCTV footage. Protecting me. Proof that I existed. I didn't have to do anything, because he'd have the evidence that I was real. I'd be grateful for it one day. I never took the time to sit next to him, though, at family parties and stuff and say hello and ask how he was in case he embarrassed me in front of my friends.

I'm not good in pictures. But I always wanted him there. Always was grateful.

Always wanted to feel small again in the spare room, tucked under the sheets, waiting for the next day when we would always do something fun.

But now I feel he can't even really look at me properly without welling up.

His tears are like glue. Thick glue.

9.

WHAT ARE WE GOING TO DO TODAY?

11.

He is a bit older than my dad. But age doesn't beat time.

Sparky's actual real-life job is an electrician and Sparky is his nickname. Maybe that's why his hair is so silver and static, always standing on end? As though he constantly has a current of electricity whipping through his bloodstream. And big blue bug eyes that are always wet. Like the glue, remember? Fish eyes, kind of. Dad once showed me photos of Sparky when he was younger. When the eyes were even bigger and wilder and the grin more frenzied. The heart probably just as big. Even then, when nothing mattered as much and there was so much less to lose.

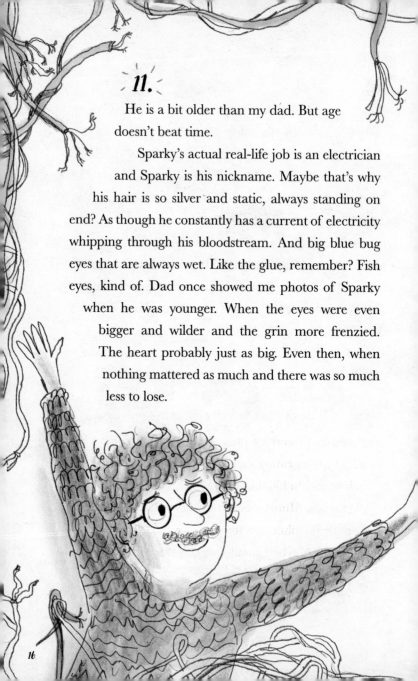

12.

I saw Sparky a bit then at the end, at the strange place with the screechy floor and the itchy blue blanket and the scone with the burnt raisins that hit my plate like a chunk of moon rock and went down my throat like rubber from a car tyre that I had to eat because 'You should try to eat something, Rex.'

And everybody was too old. Way older than my dad. But good, so they should be, that's how it's meant to go. That's how I knew it was the other way round. That's how I knew Dad was actually too young. That's how I knew it was daylight robbery.

That he'd been stolen too soon. Right underneath our noses.

Dad. Dad. Dad.

I knew Sparky wanted to talk to me but we never did. And there were no photographs taken that day. He didn't bring his camera out. Not once.

How do you file this, then?

What was Mum meant to do? Leave the photos of Dad by the plums on the kitchen table?

Maybe I should have drawn him?

Eugh. I feel horrible.

How are you? How are you doing?

I wormed out of conversation every time. And Sparky would try to catch me like a spider. But I'd be too quick.

Now I'm so slow. And I've given in.

Caught. I'm just like the bugs behind the glass. And there's nowhere to run to. It's like I'm growing backwards.

And Sparky moves so quick. As quick as a flash.

My eyes get tired and wired just from watching him.

How does he have so much energy?

He's the child and I'm the man.

I can't even pull myself out of –

13.

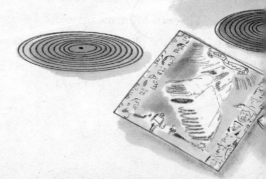

☛ *Do you want to see the first ever record your dad lent me?*

🌀 *'K then.*

14.

I'm worried because drawing doesn't work.

It doesn't make me feel good like it used to. It makes me feel worse and more broken because I can't get to it. It's out of my reach.

I draw a road from memory. The street lamps bowing down their heads in prayer, each a spot light on a stage.

I don't know this area. Or the people. Or the stuff that comes with it. I never thought I'd live here or whatever, have my own towel here. A toothbrush.

It was like I always knew this place was special but I didn't think it would be a place I'd call home.

I feel miles and miles and a universe away from the world I know. But Mum said it was too messy where we live. Everything was a reminder. Everything was too strong. Everybody kept asking. And Lottie was only four and didn't understand.

And there were traps, everywhere.

Mum said it would be good for me here; Sparky would take care of me so I could get some peace and 'feel better'. To give her space while she *dealt* with what needed to be *dealt* with.

But also it was because she couldn't *deal* with me.

'Cheer up.'

'You don't help yourself.'

'Stop moping around the place like a goth.'

I don't mind. I like nature, it's cool to draw, and Sparky lives near lots of it . . . But actually I don't know if I do like nature any more because, well . . . that was then and this is now.

I'm different.

OK . . . well . . . I guess what I'm trying to say is . . . I don't want to know nature because nature does bad things too. Like wither and tire and infect and steal away people you love for no good reason whatsoever.

Stupid dumb nature. Whose idea was that?

15.

Sparky has a garden with millions of tadpoles that glow like neon lanterns each year. One day these teensy ink beads magically turn into capers, then frogs, hoppy things with legs, and then round and around it happens over and over again. You can't tell who is who.

Sprog. Sprog. Sprog.

We could go to the park and see the deer? They'll be rutting at this time of year.

We'd always go there when I was young and I loved it.

The grass was so strong and yellow like straw, so brittle, as though it had been singed in some terrible fire, but that was just its character. It felt almost cowboy-like, a scene from the past. The trees were mountain giants unearthed on the uneven ground and you could picture their roots spreading out to distant lands, sipping water from the sea.

The silver squirrels were bushy-tailed and scuttled and scaled branches, nut-heavy, and crows pecked at picnics, snatching grey veiny things off chicken legs.

I liked it a lot. You could get lost.

I'd go with Sparky. He'd show me how to take photographs on his posh heavy camera. He would loop the camera strap over my head and I'd feel as though I was being knighted, it was such an honour to wear his camera.

We'd take traffic-light jam tarts with

shiny stained-glass-window tops that left proof of your fingerprints and drink ginger beer and pick blackberries, and nobody at school ever believed that I'd have weekends like this in London that were so wild and different.

I'd like the purple stains to stay on my clothes and fingertips as evidence to mark my adventures.

I go somewhere different, guys. I go somewhere else. Somewhere wild . . . somewhere YOU wouldn't understand . . .

I got lost.

But I don't want to go today.

Why would I want to get any *more* lost than I already am?

When I am so lost already?

Why don't I just let you be then?

I don't answer because I don't know yet if I prefer it on my own or not because I haven't had a chance to try it out yet.

OK. Well . . . I'll be downstairs . . .

I draw antlers.

11.

That night I couldn't sleep.

Even though my muscles were poisoning me with desperate tiredness and were so heavy, like parts of a dismantled aeroplane, my mind was whirling around and rushing.

I tossed and turned and flapped in the cramping darkness where time either stood exactly still or rushed past like speeding cars. I knew that the next day I'd be even more tired than the day before and my body might let me down and I'd never sleep again and get more ill and I wouldn't have the energy to repair myself.

I thought about him. And what had happened. And what I'd done.

Over and over and over again. About the grey scarf he wore. About how cold he always was. About how the heating always had to be on boiling hot because his bones were shivering like ice. Like the climbing frame in the park in winter when it's ghost-cold.

But it was so hot in our house. How could he be cold? And that heat made us irritable and snap at silly things. And Lottie wouldn't stop crying. The house was a pressure cooker and we were trapped, faces up against the glass, like starfish screwed to the

windows of a greenhouse. Mum was angry and a new person that I wasn't sure of and sometimes shouted or sometimes ignored me when I called her and even did a bit of smoking. And Lottie would cry and cry and cry all night long. And some days the milk was like cheese and there was no bread and I had to go to school with three sandy digestive biscuits crumbling away in my pocket for breakfast. And the neighbours were terrified of being asked for favour after favour so they began to walk ahead. Pretend not to see us. And I'd know he'd be up there in that drowning room all day. Alone. Forgetting himself. His legs were bloated and swollen and he wouldn't let us touch them. Or even see them. And the rich smell of sickening vanilla candles flickering to mask the thickness and the stains on the carpet and the overpowering aftershave and the ripe horrible

always sad smell
of saying goodbye

to somebody you don't ever want to say goodbye to.

And I hated it that these were the memories I had of somebody I so badly wanted to remember.

And I wanted him to stick around for ever, but at the same time I wanted it to be over.

And I felt terrible for that.

18.

I can only eat like I'm recovering from food poisoning. Potatoes and toast and plain boiled rice.

He liked those frozen yoghurt tube things that we used to love. I hate them now.

Sparky doesn't stop moving. Not even to breathe.

Flicker.

Flicker.

Hiss. Hiss.

Snap.

Beetle.

Bumble.

Scramble.

Scurry. Scurry.

Zap.
Zap.
Zap.

20.

The days drag and drag. I miss my friends. I miss my road and the bike track. I miss the familiar orange glow of the street lamp and the sirens at night. I miss school. Yes, even school. The way our house rumbles when a train flies past on the tracks and the scampering of wet city rats. I don't even know if there were any rats but I liked to imagine them, terrorising the gutters like they were meant to.

Here there is nothing but the buzz of nature, but the stars.

The swelling sky.

Silence.

I think I miss myself. Yeah. I do.

Is that possible? Is that vain?

I don't think I'll ever get back to me.

'It's just a part of growing up. It's a phase. It happens to all teenagers.'

No, it isn't. If it was, nobody would grow up, ever.

Maybe this is what old people talk about when they say life is hard. It's not the newspapers and the tax bills – it's THIS. It's becoming terrified of losing you. The happy you. The you that knows how to make decisions. That has instinct.

It's like my well of happiness . . . is empty . . . I used it all up . . . and I don't know how to get more and fill it up again . . .

I just want to feel young again. Like other kids.

And free.

I want to feel free.

21.

I feel Dad's music pumping through my veins. He used to play music so loudly, blowing the speakers until the fronts nearly popped off. Music floods through my ears no matter what side I turn on the pillow . . . or is it my own heartbeat pumping blood around me?

How do you turn off your own heart sound without dying?

The lyrics in songs mean new things to me now. They try to join together to create answers to questions I didn't even know I had before this.

It's so cryptic. And trapping.

Were they trying to tell me something all along? I'm scared of what happens next.

Where do people go?

22.

It is a Tuesday when the sun finally comes out and I feel ready to maybe see the world dressed in autumn outside. Defrosting from the warp of time.

I could try . . .

I take out my sketch book and draw . . .

Waxy big fresh green palms like dinner plates and snarling roots and purple blooms and satin soft mouths of fruits and petals like smiling lips and pollen heads fluffy like apricots and the ground, slick and papered with the camouflage swamp of crusty fallen leaves of orange and brown and red and green. Curling honey-coloured leaves hidden from the wet like battered cod, crispy and rolled up like cigars. Toad-green oval leaves, tips scarlet, veins like maps to little roads, wet with the syrup of season. The grass dusted like a floured cake with smart conkers. The splatter of rotting worm-torn, half-made apples that are speckled in freckles, blushing in red and yellow. The air smells damp and fresh, of wet wood and the mushy cloy of brewing cider. There are bugs and birds and winged things like dragonflies and the garden is magical and reminds me that maybe the world can still turn through nature. The grass is long and happy. The exact way grass should be. And surrounding it are tall bushes and stems and tangles of nettles and herbs.

There is the willow: velvet-rich curtains, hairy like dreadlocks, the arc of the tree – a bending teapot, cowering to its knees. Its bark blasted with age and effort, its stories wide . . . It has watched me grow up.

But I know what hides behind it. And I can't go in.

And I U-turn as soon as I imagine myself doing so . . .

And I look up to see Sparky at the back door from the kitchen give that smile to me that wants to be tears.

   It's OK.

23.

From that day forward Sparky tries to make almost everything happen in the garden. He says the outdoors is good for us.

We move the sofa out, wire up the speakers and set them up outside with lamps and fairy lights and festoons – the heavy white sky is lit up and lifted by glowing twinkles and I'm maybe happy for a moment and ALMOST able to forget, but then a fuse pops and there's a **blackout**

Ah. Crumbs.

24.

– but the light comes back again. And so does the music. And the thoughts.

While Sparky busily sorts trunks of wires and bulbs and bolts and screws and mutters about how good it is to get all these little jobs done, I sit next to him and try to read some of the books I've been given from school or draw or watch the tops of houses, the moss and the cables in the sky, the chimney pots and dots of planes passing. I think about the people inside. Going to new places. Going home. Excited. How everything is normal-sized to them but they look tiny to me now and I look tiny to them too.

Wow. Life just goes on for everybody, doesn't it? Just like a plane. It doesn't stop and wait for you.

If the people in the plane spotted us in the garden, they'd see me and Sparky. In silence. Wearing worn-out holey jumpers and drinking strong tea.

⚡ *Didn't you want to have children, Sparky?*

🍫 *I've got you, haven't I? You're more than enough.*

⚡ *Why are you being so kind to me?*

🍫 *Because I promised I would. You can always fall back on me, Rex. And I will always keep that promise.*

Our tea is going cold.

🍫 *I'll get some more tea on . . . Sneaky sugar?*

⚡ *Go on then.*

I nod. Sparky winks. And his bofty soles creep towards the back door where the kitchen is.

The air whips up, making leaves pirouette and skittle past. The willow's arms swing like apes, and I catch a peep of it.

Thump. Thump. Thump.

I know I'm not ready. It is the last place I want to go on the whole Earth.

Oh no, my head is the last place, this is one before that.

25.

We go around in the electrician van, which I like. We listen to good music and have cheese and pickle rolls with salt and vinegar crisps stuffed inside.

Crunch.
Crunch.
Crunch.

I manage to stomach food more on the go, when it accidentally goes down without much fuss and I am distracted. We go to Sparky's jobs and he tells me all the gossip about each customer, like how Mrs Munroe once stole a white dog, dyed the fur pink and then returned it to the owner.

⚡ *Why?*

☛ *She just had to get it out of her system, I suppose.*

Sparky never asked me if I was into electricity or not. I never really thought about it, though obviously I appreciate it, light and warmth. Can you be *into* electricity? What do we have in common? Maybe Sparky and I are opposites, like a − and +.

Sparky once unscrewed a plug and said:

☛ *Hey, you can draw the inside of the plug . . .*

He went on to show me the wires and I began to draw the open-heart surgery in a little plastic body.

☛ *Here's a tip for you . . .*

And then he told me the 'tip'. This time it was:

☛ *Always wear rubber soles when you touch electricity. It can stop the shock.*

But I don't think that is true for the type of shock that I am feeling.

26.

On Friday I felt tired and decided to ride the wave. I was so sure that the second my head smashed into the pillow I'd be wrapped up in a cocoon of deep peace. That my body would fall into the warmth and folds and flesh of my bed and sink me away, slip me to another dream place where the bad stuff didn't exist and nothing really mattered . . .

But my eyes wouldn't

stick

and the bed was **too hot**

and the pressing on my chest too deep and heavy, and my mind waltzed and wavered and played evil horrendous tricks on me and my tummy ached, knotted and cramped and released and I had to go to the toilet AGAIN for a millionth wee and I gagged and nagged and my jaw was clenched so tight it felt like it was a short elastic band and my teeth felt shattered like broken china cups and I was sweating and thirsty and my mouth tasted sour like a goldfish bowl and the—clock—was—an—endless hollow pit. A bully.

And I wasn't scared of the monster under the bed like I was back when I was small.

My fears are new fears.

Ahhh . . . this must be how you grow out of ghosts. Something terrible happens in real life and then the stuff you dream up in horror dreams suddenly dissolves.

Why doesn't it happen like it does in the films? There are no sirens. There are no red and blue flashing lights. Nobody gets in trouble.

There is nobody to blame. Maybe there is.

I can't tell any more.

27.

It was the longest, slowest rip in the world, one that just kept on tearing and tearing and tearing . . .

I'm falling.

I'm falling.

I'm falling.

I'm drowning.

I'm drowning.

I'm drowning.

28.

I was scared of somebody I loved because they weren't being the same any more and I didn't know how to be or what to say or do and I'd shout at him when he'd forget important things about me or not come to football or look at my drawings because he'd have drifted off to sleep by the time I got my book and we weren't growing apart like how everybody said we would; no, we were two trees strangling each other, sucking the breath away.

Dad, you think of me as angry and scared. Well, I think of you as scary and scared.

All I could do was be afraid of the one person who usually kept me safe even when they were scared of themselves too.

And I can't even go and climb into bed with Sparky because that would feel dumb and babyish and I want him to think I am all grown-up now and fine.

I want him to think I am brave.

And then I realise that perhaps I am still scared of ghosts. I was terrified of my dad.

With no sleep I am a zombie with puffy eyes and a screw-loose mind and I am clumsy and spill tea down myself.

Sparky says the sunshine has come out for *me* and if I can't sleep I don't need to worry, he's got me decaffeinated teabags. He says the sun could help charge my batteries and I help him move the sofa outside again and I charge up like a mobile phone.

We sit and listen to the radio. People talk about the economy and everybody is posh and baby spiders chase up my arms in tickles but I don't mind. With a blanket wrapped round me like wings I feel my eyes close and sleep tugging itself round me like a rowing-boat-shaped cloud drifting off into space.

And I fall asleep.

I dream of him. Of him pretending to take his hands off the wheel when we were driving. He'd say . . . 'HOLD ON . . . WE'RE GONNA CRASH, I HOPE YOU CAN DRIVE, REX!'

And when he'd pick me up in my pyjamas and throw me into the bath fully clothed and stroke my head and buy me books and pretend to steal my nose and put it in his pocket or walk into lamp posts.

I dream of him drumming teaspoons on the coffee

pot while the kettle grumbles noisily behind. He'd pout his lips out like he was a rock star, the worn spoon an electric guitar.

He put baked beans with everything.

I dream of his smell: aftershave and newspapers and beer. His favourite time to eat chocolate was first thing in the morning even though that's the time you're definitely NOT meant to be eating chocolate. He carried photographs of me and Lottie in his wallet.

And how he'd laugh so hard he would giggle like a child and his silver sardine-coloured fillings would flash like bullets.

He loved words and would ask me what I thought the lyrics in songs meant:

Did they hit my heart?

Did they make sense?

He'd tell me the backstory behind them even if they were explicit or not stuff a grown-up would usually tell a kid. He wanted me to learn; he was interested in the world. He'd make up songs for me too and he didn't need to explain the meanings behind them because I knew what they were about. Even if they were just about his big toe. Or the annoying woman who worked at the desk at school with the weird eyebrows.

30.

I go to draw an aeroplane but I write in my sketchbook.

Dad,

I feel like I have to tell you I miss you but you're not here to tell. I'm sorry I was scared of you but you didn't look like you. That's why I couldn't give you a hug like how I wanted to. I don't know why I did that to you. I'm sorry I let you go with me looking at you like that.

I'm sorry for what I did. I'm sorry for it all.

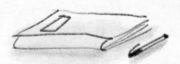

🗲 *Oi!*

⚡ *Huh?*

I wake with a startle.

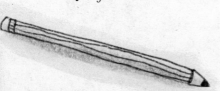

🗲 Helllloooooo!

The voice goes again . . .

⚡ *Who's that?*

🗲 *Why aren't you ever at school?*

⚡ *Me?*

🗲 *Nahhhh . . . I was talking to the other invisible lad sleeping in the garden.*

⚡ *It's not a school day.*

🗲 *Yeah, but you haven't been at school all week.*

I shrug.

🗲 *I don't go to school either.*

⚡ *Why?*

🗲 *It's rude to answer a question with a question.*

⚡ *I just don't.*

    ✄ *What, do you just live here now then?*

    ♧ *It's not for ever.*

    ✄ *Oh, I KNOW that.*

Is he challenging me?

    ♧ *How?*

    ✄ *Because nothing is for ever.*

I try peering through a gap in the fence but I can't see anything. I don't like the idea of him – this anonymous voice – having the advantage of seeing me but me not being able to see him. It feels all creepy.

He speaks again . . .

    ✄ *So why is the sofa outside? Is he mad, that man you live with? He left you a note there. See?*

He is right. Sparky has left me a note. I read it in my head.

Rex,
Popped out to shops! Didn't want
to wake you. Won't be a min.
Sparky

💠 *He's not mad . . . Don't say he's mad. He's kind of mad,
but only in a good way that you'd want to be. He's like my
uncle . . . and the sofa is outside because he wants me to be
outside more.*

📣 *Sounds pretty mad to me but 'K. Whatever.*

He is starting to annoy me. I pick up my mug and
begin to walk back into the house. I don't
need this weird kid from behind a fence
asking me a batrillion questions. I'm not
in the mood.

🔊 *What's your name?*

I stop and turn round . . .

🕊 *What's yours?*

🔊 *See, again, rude. Very rude.*

🕊 *Rex.*

🔊 *That's a dog's name.*

🕊 *That's rude.*

🔊 *No, that's honesty. That's completely different.*

🕊 *Well, what's your name then?*

🔊 *Sidney.*

🕊 *Well, that's a girls' name.*

🔊 *No, it isn't.*

🕊 *I'm going inside. Catch you later maybe.*

🔊 *What do you do all day? You can tell me; I won't tell anyone. Are you on the run?*

He is not giving up.

🕊 *No.*

🔊 *If you are, that's totally cool. I just want to know.*

🕊 *I'm not on the run.*

🔊 *Are you hiding from villains or baddies or gangsters or*

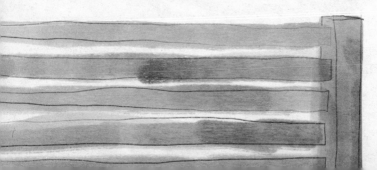

whatever? You can tell me; I won't tell a soul. I once kept a secret that my mum broke my gran's expensive antique vase and replaced it with this cheap old thing and I never told anybody that ever. Well. Except for you. Oh. But that was just to demonstrate that I can actually keep secrets. So that doesn't count. But if I didn't tell you an actual secret, how would you know for yourself if I was actually any good at it? See, had to be legit.

   ⚜ *I don't have a secret.*

   🗲 *Everybody has a secret. That's what makes us different from animals. Animals can't keep secrets.*

   ⚜ *They see stuff, though.*

   🗲 *Duhhh . . . Even the leaves see stuff. Even the air. Have you done something?*

   ⚜ *NO!*

I hear the crack of the back door opening, Sparky calling my name . . .

REX!

He is home.

And the rustle of the bushes behind the fence shudders and there is the sound of feet scurrying away . . .

They only had one chocolate croissant, so I got a plain and an almond and we can share –

Where's he gone?

Who?

He was just there . . .

Who?

I squint out into the distance.

No one. Just a bird.

Sparky looks at me, his eyes watering. He is 'sensitive' too like that. Sometimes it annoyed Dad. They'd go to watch bands together and Dad would come back and Mum would say:

How was it?

and Dad would say:

Sparky cried the whole way through again!

And Mum would laugh affectionately.

He places a warm paw on my shoulder; his fingertips are rough and worn and swollen from working, fiddling with screws, getting nipped and burned.

You're tired, Rex. You're going to see him in places because he never left you. He's been around your whole life; he's not going to just one day disappear.

No, it was a bird.

It's always my worst part in films and stuff when the grown-ups never believe the kids. They might see a howling wolf or a vampire or a monster and they run home to tell their parents or whatever and the monster ALWAYS, guaranteed, every time, never, ever, ever shows its face when the adult is around. Ever. And I hate that. It used to make me so mad. Not that Sidney is a monster. He's just annoying. But still.

33.

Mum calls. She says Lottie wants to say hello but Lottie doesn't want to say hello at all. She just wants to talk about Peppa Pig and the fairy cakes with hundreds and thousands she made. Even Lottie has more going on than me these days.

Mum says she misses me and I can come home now if I want to. I say I'll stay one more night and think about it. I tell her I miss her too.

🎵 *It's all just been such a lot.*

She exhales. She is crying but trying to fight it.

I advise her to wear shoes with rubber soles to help with the shock.

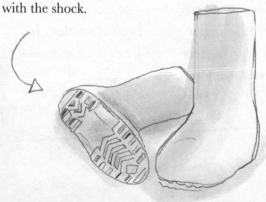

And how are you . . . feeling?

I tell her I'm fine.

I don't tell her about the heaviness
on my chest or the cramps or the aches
or the sickness or the sleeplessness or
the numbness or the lack of appetite.

I DON'T tell her about Sidney.

Have you been eating?

I lie.

Yes. I've been eating.

I go back into the kitchen and reach for the little
white paper bag and bite the end of my croissant.

It's actually OK.

34.

It's Monday. Sidney doesn't come back. I try to train my ears to tune into the quietest of noises in case I hear him treading around behind the fence. Rustling about spying on me. But nothing.

The breeze plays the trees like a harp. Maybe he decided to go to school?

Maybe he lied about not going to school? Maybe he's just a liar?

I draw . . .

The rain patters, banging the flowerpots and watering cans,

snails trawl,

stringy long-legged bugs abseil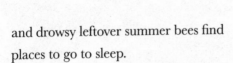

and drowsy leftover summer bees find
places to go to sleep.

And autumn comes along properly
now, in one red-and-orange blustering
sweep.

Sidney's fence is too high for me
to see into his garden. His curtains are
closed.

Maybe I'll stay just one more day.

35.

Sleep is still so close yet so far, calling my name but in a muffled voice, and I always go in the wrong direction into awake land.

I have an idea.

36.

As soon as the light comes, the sun turning into a new day, a crack of bleached-out silver, I creep down the stairs. There are crumbs on the side and a mug of tea from Sparky, left out from the night before. The tea has a ghost of white skin on top from where it's been left overnight.

There are photos of *him* too. I think from when they were young but I don't touch them or even look because I know what they are for. He's trying to find happy ones. Ones where he is smiling. And they are sort of hidden underneath the boring newspapers, deliberately, so I don't see. Not that it's a secret. Not that anything has to be hidden from me to know it's real.

I twist the doorknob softly soft, but it still moans and I have no shoes on and my feet feel cold. But I reckon if I don't do this now, I might never, and you have to listen to the voice that makes you do the things you think you're scared of sometimes. Sometimes the quieter voice is the one with the strongest thing to say; it's just that we've turned the volume down in our heads.

The wet grass is keen to know my toes and shoots up in blades underneath my skin. Morning birds chirp.

I know the way. I know the way.

Past the pond with the squirming spawning ripeness. Creep round, down and under, where the ground becomes denser and bark chips fall beneath every step and the holly bush lets you squeeze past even though she's fat and overgrown and wants to stick to your clothes and scratch you. But she never does. Somebody else she might, but never you. Her thorns, like upturned plugs, try to trap me, but I slide the arches of my feet to the side.

Past the shimmering cobwebs, adorned with gemstones of dew and under the willow tree with its sunken head.

Here the soil loosens, flattens and the bushes twist and corridor, winding. I duck under the canopy of swooping branches, the tentacles of hairy green dangle. The earth is soft and sand-like.

Welcome back, Rex. Welcome back.

37.

I pause a moment before flicking the latch. Thumbing for the familiar groove. It's black paint, orangey, rusted and worn. An oval of paint cracks off when I press, and crumbles away in my hand like ash. Cobwebs knit together around the lip of the door and veiny ivy seems to have clung to the wooden walls. The sign is still there; though weather-worn it has kept its shape, the drawing pins speckled with a pink rash but the words still readable.

I take a breath.

38.

🖎 *What are you doing?*

I see an eye peep through a crack in the fence. It's green.

🗝 *Sidney . . . Where have you been?*

🖎 *Waiting for you. Obviously.*

🗝 *I looked for you. You never came back.*

🖎 *Well, I'm here now, aren't I?*

🗝 *It's early.*

🖎 *Tell me about it. What are you doing?*

I did think it was odd that he was awake too. Although sometimes when I have a rough night's sleep I realise later that lots of other people have also had rough night's sleep . . . like maybe it's to do with the moon or something? Or the sky? Change of season? Bolts of current shooting through the earth?

🗝 *You couldn't sleep either?*

🖎 *I don't ever sleep good.*

🗝 *I wanted to show you something.*

He peers over. His brows rise.

🖎 *What? A shed?*

🗝 *No. It's got a window, look, and more . . . inside.*

🖎 *Hold on then. Let's see.*

Sidney stands back and takes a run, his foot batters Sparky's fence from the other side with a kick as he ambles up. The ivy and willow rattle as a pair of little scratched knuckles and dirty fingernails grip the top of the fence. The wisteria above trembles. Then, followed by a beaten-up, once-white tennis trainer, is a head with a scruff of dark black hair. Sidney grins as he hauls himself over, proud, the fence wavering beneath him. The moss making his hands slip. Then he lands, two feet proudly next to mine. The fallen leaves crunch.

He's bony. Scruffy.

His clothes are weird. A bit like he's raided some sort of charity shop bargain bucket and is about to go on to help a friend paint a spare room. It's almost as though he isn't really sure of what he has on himself. A bobbly red-wine T-shirt and strange almost-school-uniform-grey trousers that he sort of pulls off in some odd way.

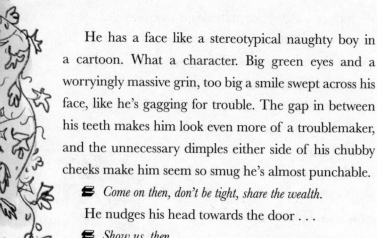

He has a face like a stereotypical naughty boy in a cartoon. What a character. Big green eyes and a worryingly massive grin, too big a smile swept across his face, like he's gagging for trouble. The gap in between his teeth makes him look even more of a troublemaker, and the unnecessary dimples either side of his chubby cheeks make him seem so smug he's almost punchable.

Come on then, don't be tight, share the wealth.

He nudges his head towards the door . . .

Show us, then.

I hesitate. I don't know if Sparky would be happy to see the boy from behind the fence here in his garden.

'K. But you know what you said about the animals . . . and us . . . and keeping secrets?

I am well good at keeping secrets.

Well, this is one secret that can't be used as an example.

I thought you didn't have a secret.

Promise?

Promise. So . . . are we, like, going in then?

I don't know why I feel so nervous. My body is tingling with fear. The door has a beating heart, pulsing

through my veins and wrapping round my grip. Its
tremor strikes my bones. It's like he's watching me, Dad,
urging me to step inside . . .

🖘 *Are you OK?*

🗲 *I can't. I . . . just . . . sorry.*

I back away towards the house.

🖘 *You can just say. I can keep secrets, you know. Oi, you
don't have to run. If you don't want me to go inside, you can
just say. Don't have to be a chicken or whatever . . . It's ONLY
a PLACE!*

I twist the doorknob to the kitchen door. Hit by the
familiar smell of Sparky's. The faint smell of wood,
antiques and burnt toast. The door closed, I release.
Only a place? He knows nothing. He certainly doesn't
know me.

I watch Sidney hop back over the fence the way he
came.

The garden rustles and then conceals his route . . .
as though he was never even there at all.

39.

🖢 *I wouldn't call it a quiche. Would you? The recipe says quiche but it's more tart-like.*

I shrug. I don't know the difference.

🖢 *It's from this old vegetarian food magazine. I'm probably the only person in the world that still uses the recipes. It doesn't even look like it's meant to in the picture.*

I wish we could get Deliveroo.

He cuts into the tart. I watch him watching me and force a crumb into my mouth.

♧ *It tastes good to me.*

It's potato-y, cheesy, herby.

🖢 *That's the point, I suppose. Looks a mess, though. I don't do enough cooking. It's nice to have someone to cook for.*

He steps up; his knees crack.

🖢 *Splodge of ketchup wouldn't hurt, though, would it?*

He steps up to the cupboard.

🖢 *Oh, crumbs. We're out of tomato sauce.*

I didn't fancy it until he said it. Now I'm craving tomato sauce more than ever. And then the power cuts.

- Oh, crumbs!

Plunging the two of us into thick darkness. It immediately makes the kitchen feel smaller, like the furniture is crowding round us, alive, with arms that want to draw us in. A tickle creeps up my spine and my hair stands on end.

Why does it feel like we aren't alone?

The pair of us sit in darkness. I expect Sparky to get up and fix it but he doesn't. We just sit in the darkness, knives and forks scratching away at the plate.

- *Tastes even better when you can't see it.*

Sparky jokes and I like hearing his voice break the emptiness.

I like the way he always sees the good in everything.

I look out to the dark garden, nature sleeping, the pond, a lacquer of bubbling witches' brew reflecting in the glass to the Dream House. And I'm almost certain I see a shade of a figure shuffling about inside.

I knew I couldn't trust him.

40.

That night. I watch from my bedroom window. The Dream House. But nothing happens. The willow's arms spring about like hairy Tarzan ropes in the breeze, sweeping the leafy floor like octopus-tentacle broomsticks. I glare with penetration at the little wooden house, almost hoping to see the figure again, to catch them in the act.

Not that I need to guess who it is.

I know who it is. It's Sidney. I know it is.

My eyes begin to play tricks and paint pictures in the darkness, creating shadows that morph and twitch. And when the silence shrouds the garden, I feel my eyelids get heavy and at last I give into sleep.

I'VE BEEN WAITING FOR YOU.

41.

Mum calls bright and early. She and Lottie were thinking of coming to collect me. 'We miss our boy,' they say, and Mum adds, 'Don't we?' to Lottie and she replies with a gargled, 'Who is a boy?'

I tell her I don't want collecting. I want to spend a bit more time here if that is OK. She suggests coming to see me with Lottie. We could go for a pub lunch.

I say not today. Maybe another day.

'Are you sure you don't want to come home now? Your friends have been asking after you.'

I say, 'Just a little while longer.'

Then she talks to Sparky for ages and I watch the rain run tears down the windows. How it flicks the leaves outside and hangs heavy on the plants.

42.

I go outside later on, peeling a tangerine, its skin coming off in shapes like bits of an atlas. I go towards the Dream House, this time stepping over the itchy grass, peering into the window.

Then his voice . . .

🝰 *Why are you being like this?*

🝰 *Like what?*

I am annoyed and I want him to know.

🝰 *All . . . Gah, you know what I mean, man. It's just a shed.*

🝰 *It's not.*

🝰 *Looks like one of them normal ones. I s'pose, though, it's what's on the inside that counts, isn't it?*

🝰 *You should know.*

I stab.

🝰 *How should I?*

Intruder.

🝰 *Look, it's one thing to go inside without me, without even ASKING permission, but then to go ahead and lie about it too!*

Sidney looks baffled.

🝰 *Lie? I didn't lie and I didn't go in your little shed thing either. What makes you think I would go in there!*

🝰 *I saw you.*

⚡ *When?*

✦ *Last night.*

⚡ *Impossible.*

✦ *Where were you then?*

⚡ *Er. That's not your business, but I wasn't in your shed.*

✦ *It's not a shed. Stop calling it a 'shed'.*

⚡ *Whatever it is. I wasn't in there! Why don't you believe me?*

✦ *Because I don't even know you. As far as I'm concerned you're just a kid from the other side of the fence. And maybe you've been using this as your own secret hiding den for a while, thinking it was derelict and neglected . . . and now I'm back, I'm here, and you've realised that it's not yours. That it belongs to me.*

⚡ *What are you on about? I've never even been in there.*

✦ *OK, so maybe you're planning on taking it over once I've gone back home? Well, that's not happening.*

I don't even know if I believe any of the stuff I am saying but I am so angry it is just pouring out.

⚡ *Why would I try and take over some shed in the back of some nutcase's garden? You're mental, mate; you've lost the plot.*

✦ *Oh, OK. Have I? Unbelievable.*

⚡ *Look, you were the one that wanted to show it to me; it's not my fault you got scared and ran off.*

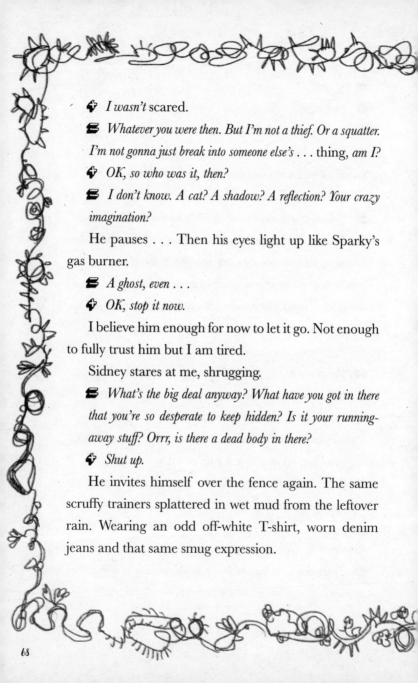

♣ *I wasn't* scared.

☙ *Whatever you were then. But I'm not a thief. Or a squatter.*
I'm not gonna just break into someone else's . . . thing, am I?

♣ *OK, so who was it, then?*

☙ *I don't know. A cat? A shadow? A reflection? Your crazy*
imagination?

He pauses . . . Then his eyes light up like Sparky's
gas burner.

☙ *A ghost, even . . .*

♣ *OK, stop it now.*

I believe him enough for now to let it go. Not enough
to fully trust him but I am tired.

Sidney stares at me, shrugging.

☙ *What's the big deal anyway? What have you got in there*
that you're so desperate to keep hidden? Is it your running-
away stuff? Orrr, is there a dead body in there?

♣ *Shut up.*

He invites himself over the fence again. The same
scruffy trainers splattered in wet mud from the leftover
rain. Wearing an odd off-white T-shirt, worn denim
jeans and that same smug expression.

🖤 Yeah, cos if someone got murdered for, like . . . I dunno . . . some insane crime, well, actually this shed thing would be a proper good place to hide in cos that tree thing covers it. Not got an address or anything. Who'd even know it exists?

⚡ Yeah, but no murderers know it exists either, do they?

🖤 Yeah, but, see, now how do you know who is and who isn't a murderer, mate, though? I've seen this one thing on TV, yeah, where this nutter man – well, actually he seemed normal; he liked cereal and wore a suit and stuff, but he must have been a nutter cos then he just went on some murdering spree in his sleep. He didn't even know he was doing it. Proper mad, isn't it? That's why I always sleep with my hands crossed over together like this, so I can check I haven't moved in the night and gone and killed someone. And if you did want to hide a body in there, if the police did even get close to finding it, you could suddenly just burn it down, couldn't you? So what is in there then? Lawnmowers and paint and that?

⚡ No!

🖤 Like, what's it for then?

I don't answer. Don't want to say what it is actually for. What it was built for. 'Dreaming' basically. Inventing, playing . . . passing time.

📚 *Very, very mysterious anyway. Who made it?*

🔱 *Sparky . . . and my dad.*

📚 *Where is your dad anyway?*

I change the subject.

🔱 *So, do you want to look inside or what?*

📚 *Only if you like . . . cos, like, yeah, I do, but, like, I also don't know what's in there cos you're acting a bit, I dunno . . . off about the whole thing, like there's gonna be some mad monster freak type thing in there and I just . . . only if you think . . .*

❧ *Nobody has ever been in here before other than me. And obviously Sparky. And neither of us has been inside for absolutely years.*

❧ *Oh, so I should be acting like this is a really big deal and everything?*

❧ *Yeah. Well. It kind of is a big deal.*

Sidney licks his palm and flattens his hair down, smoothing it around his ears, as though he is about to meet the Queen.

He shakes his head, annoyed, and says:

❧ *I knew I should have worn my backwards cap.*

43.

We step up to the door. Me at the front, of course. That same heartbeat begins to pulsate through me. Currents penetrating. Like the house and I are connected somehow. Almost as if, if I touch the catch, I'd get a sharp electric shock.

Maybe I should have done this on my own, for the first time at least.

Get it out the way . . . break the seal, familiarise myself . . . but then I quite like the presence of Sidney, the company . . . He knows how to break the ice.

🖅 *Why's it say 'Dream House' then? That's kind of –*

✤ *What?*

🖅 *No, no, nothing.*

✤ *If you're gonna be all annoying about it, Sidney, then don't come in.*

🖅 *Awwwright, awwwright . . . bit romantic, that's all. Bit . . . I dunno, gross.*

✤ *No. It's not gross! Or romantic. It's about dreams. It's . . . Yeah, OK, it does sound kind of . . . Look, it's not romantic, OK? It's magic.*

And I feel a stinging magnetic urgency to place my hand on the door and pull it open.

The door is stiff with weathered edges, worn and

oversized in its frame. Swollen from the seasons. Vines and ivy have wrapped themselves round the sides in braids and the now-battered hinges groan as I softly try to pull the door forward.

🔖 *See, no one's been in there . . . It's basically security-tagged with the amount of vines around there. How would I have got in there without you knowing?*

He does have a point.

♧ *It doesn't want to open. These plants have overgrown. Look, it won't come away.*

🔖 *Just give it a good – Here, let me . . .*

Sidney steps forward and goes to give the door a yank.

♧ *Wait, you'll pull the door off its hinges!*

🔖 *How will I?*

Sidney snaps.

🔖 *I won't. Look, trust me.*

I step back as Sidney lodges a foot in the damp earth and then yanks the door forward. The greenery tears apart, springing the door open.

I expect dust. I expect light.

A big familiar smell or sound to reach out to me and call me inside . . . but all there is, is darkness.

44.

Mum was the one who was always sick, not Dad. She'd catch every bug there was to be caught like she was building a collection. But she never complained. That was why it was such a shock that it was Dad who got ill.

That one Christmas, after Lottie had been born, when Mum was too sick to get out of bed.

Dad did me a 'posh' Christmas dinner for one. He pretended the living room was a restaurant; he set up my painting table with a sophisticated tablecloth and a

little flower in a glass. He invited me to dress up in my smart suit. He dressed up like a waiter with his fancy red tie that I hardly ever saw him in, with the fishing-hook-tackle-feather thing on it. He filled my glass with blackcurrant in a wine glass and gave me three options to choose from: beans on toast, Crunchy Nut Cornflakes or Christmas dinner (with all the trimmings). He waited, apprehensive, with his pen hovering at the ready. I knew then that I pretty much had the best dad in the world.

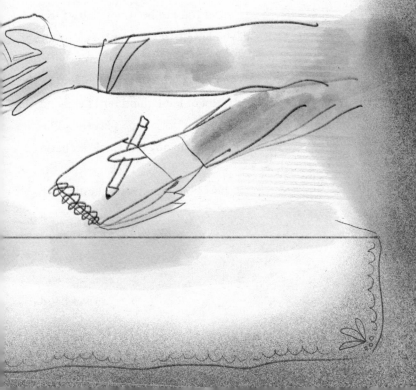

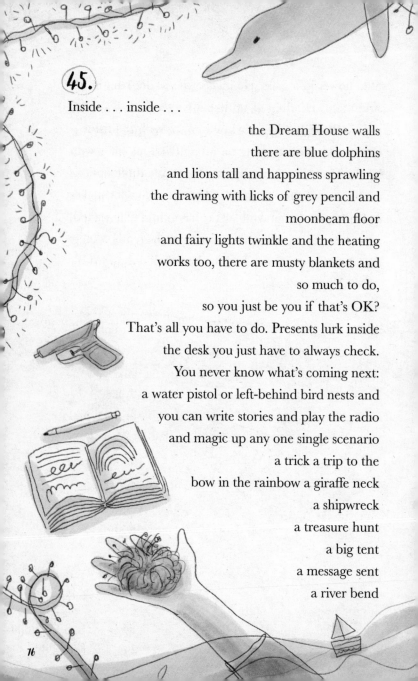

45.

Inside . . . inside . . .

the Dream House walls
there are blue dolphins
and lions tall and happiness sprawling
the drawing with licks of grey pencil and
moonbeam floor
and fairy lights twinkle and the heating
works too, there are musty blankets and
so much to do,
so you just be you if that's OK?
That's all you have to do. Presents lurk inside
the desk you just have to always check.
You never know what's coming next:
a water pistol or left-behind bird nests and
you can write stories and play the radio
and magic up any one single scenario
a trick a trip to the
bow in the rainbow a giraffe neck
a shipwreck
a treasure hunt
a big tent
a message sent
a river bend

whatever you dream up in that head.
Comfort clouds in arms around you
reassure no harm can come to you. I breathe
you softly through the fibres wherever you nestle.
Trust I'm behind you and
your tiniest thoughts will be forever safe with me
and I will tread so
delicately on your every mountain
of moments.
I will never let your heart get frozen or when the
roaring fire threatens to burn let that be none of
your concern.
I will blaze a trail of my love for you; I could
start a war or riot with my love for you.
I'm not around but in here you'll find me
And you'll feel as though it's cold right now but
you're always getting warmer. You won't have to
cower in the corner
just borrow a feeling to save another.
You just keep on believing
you're dreaming and you'll recover.

You are just dreaming.
You will recover.

46.

🐝 *What the –*

🐦 *Hang on, let me find the light . . . It should be here some—*
It's lower than I remember . . . Hold on . . .

And then it fills with light as it all comes back.

47.

Twinkling fairy lights are pinned to the walls like bunting, coloured festoon bulbs light up like candy sweets in jars; orange, pink, green, dangling, rich, in thick grey beards of cobweb and dust. The walls project shadows of strange monsters.

There are the pictures of the dolphins, the mummy and the baby one, swimming side by side, the lions – the dad one and the cub in the wilderness – my little desk. Old-fashioned. Wooden, with a big, chunky, stiff, pull-out drawer and the inkwell that always remained empty, but inside would be filled with the new stuff that Sparky would buy me for my visits: colouring books, nature books, water pistols, potato guns, pranks, a badge maker, crayons, coloured chalk, sweets, biscuits, bubblegum and reels of plain wallpaper for writing and drawing that went on for ever like scrolls from a king inviting you to a ball in a fairy tale. The presents were always old-fashioned but I liked that. It made the Dream House even more magical, like stepping back in time; I wondered what strange toyshop he even went to to get all this stuff.

The carpeted floor looks exactly the same to me as always, rough and navy with white little beard-like hairs of itchy wool looped through each line. I remember Sparky saying he had found the carpet in the skip outside an old school that was being gutted for fancy flats. I love the way the carpet is what gives the Dream House the 'house' bit of its name. It makes the house so convincing.

I can see Sidney is impressed.

🖢 *What's this?*

🐦 *A record player.*

🖢 *SICK! Let's play a record.*

🐦 *It's my dad's. Don't touch –*

BANG.

The power cuts out.

And we are plunged into darkness. The depths of the willow tree completely shroud us, heavy like theatre curtains.

🗲 *OH MY ACTUAL DAYS, REX. ARE YOU A FLICKING WIZARD?*

⚡ *No, Sid. It's called a blackout.*

🗲 *A what out?*

⚡ *You've never heard of a blackout? When the power or electricity or light just goes. It happens when a fuse blows . . . It's called a trip, I think. It's easily fixed.*

🗲 *Ow, jealous. We've never had one.*

⚡ *That's because you don't live with a crazy electrician.*

🗲 *So he is crazy?*

I throw him a dirty look.

🗲 *So, what now?*

⚡ *Well, it's too dark to see. Let's come back after Sparky fixes it. It won't take long. Should have brought my phone to light it up in here.*

🗲 *Ah, that's a shame. I really wanted to see –*

⚡ *Me too.*

🗲 *Nah, wait, I've got a little torch thingy on my keys . . . If it still works . . . What? It's from a Christmas cracker. It's cool.*

Sidney makes an effort to light up the room with the
dim little circle.

⚡ *I dunno, it doesn't look its best; you need to see it when it's
. . . Just not like this, all dark.*

⚡ *Still well good in the dark, though. What's that?*

⚡ *A stingray.*

⚡ *Looks like my sister in the mornings. And
that hanging up there?*

⚡ *It's an umbrella, from Thailand I think,
but Mum got it for me in the junk shop.*

⚡ *Can't you just fix it? The power cut?*

⚡ *No! You have to really know what you're doing.*

⚡ *But surely if you've seen Quirky do it a thousand —*

⚡ *Sparky.*

⚡ *Whatever. Sparky then. Surely you've seen him
do it?*

⚡ *No. It's dangerous.*

⚡ *Fine, be boring then.*

⚡ *Well, I don't see you fixing it.*

⚡ *This is not
my Dream House. It's
not up to me to do the
maintenance; it's yours. And
also, if I knew how, I would.*

⚡ *It's not even that hard.*

⚡ *So go do it then. Or are you too scared?*

⚡ *No. I'm not scared.*

⚡ *Do it then.*

⚡ *Fine then. I will . . . Oh no, I can't.*

⚡ *Why not now?*

⚡ *You've got to wear rubber shoes.*

⚡ *Rubber shoes? Why?*

⚡ *No, shoes with rubber soles, in case you get shocked. Electric shocked.*

⚡ *I've been electric shocked before. It's nothing.*

⚡ *Have you?*

⚡ *Yeah.*

⚡ *How?*

⚡ *Sucked the telephone wire, didn't I?*

⚡ *Huh?*

⚡ *Yeah, right up, like a straw. I thought I could drink up the power. You know, to be strong like a superhero and electrocute stuff and that with my hands.*

⚡ *Weird.*

⚡ *Ain't no other kids going round with electricity coming out their fingers. Imagine walking round with all that electric juice in your belly like WOOOOOOAHHHHHHHHHH! Hey . . . use my shoes?*

🔌 *I'm not wearing your shoes, Sidney.*

🔋 *Why not? I'm completely hygienic and always have baths and also, look, they have rubber soles, so then you won't get shocked.*

🔌 *Well, maybe . . . OK . . . What size are you?*

🔋 *What does it matter? You're only wearing them for safety.*

🔌 *Let me just put my foot up against yours then.*

🔋 *This is so unnecessary.*

🔌 *No, it isn't. I'm not undoing my laces for no reason.*

Sidney and I scramble about on the old-school carpet. We lift our feet. Our soles meet.

Hmm . . . they are rubber soles.

Sparky has taught me before: *Earth wire. Neutral wire. Live wire.* I know what a fuse looks like too.

🔌 *All right, I'll do it.*

🔋 *Wicked!*

🔌 *Give me your shoes, then.*

🔋 *Here . . .*

🔌 *They stink!*

🔋 *Liar! Let me smell . . . Hardly! Bit musty, that's all.*

🔌 *Don't touch anything.*

🔋 *I'm not. So paranoid you are. Uptight, aren't you?*

He is doing *touching*. Course he is. I can feel him

touching everything with his little curious fingers. If I was him, I would touch the stuff in the Dream House too. Still, I keep my focus. I climb on top of the desk and reach up to the little wooden box hidden in the ceiling. The desk creaks under my weight. I wouldn't have been able to reach the little electric box in the past but now I can.

This is where all the wires are kept. I try to pull the door open with my fingers.

Sidney is still waffling on below.

I don't get why somebody would just build this. Like . . . for what reason? I mean, I suppose there don't always have to be reasons, do there, but, like, it seems like quite a mad thing to do to just build *a spare little house in the garden that's just for . . . dreaming. Except there's no beds. So you can't even sleep. It's cool, though. I used to always want to build a den in my garden but there's nothing to even build a den with. It's just them boring slabs and a table with four chairs that aren't even nice to sit on. And everything is covered in bird poo. And I did want to be a spy but that never came to anything either. Spies have dens.*

85

48

With my nails, I get underneath a corner. If I could just force it . . . Sidney carries on talking . . . I want to say he is annoying me, but I find it comforting, like a radio. A really annoying radio.

I'm going to ask my dad if he'll build me something like this, then we can both have one and go to each other's 'houses' like neighbours. But I'm not calling mine anything sad like 'Dream House'. No . . . mine will be more of a Batman Cave. Maybe your dad and that Sparky could help me, seeing as they've already done this place and got experience under their belts . . . Where'd you say your dad was again?

And then, suddenly, the door to the electric box springs open and there's a squawking, flapping panic as sharp black silky beating wings scratch out of the panelling. A bat? A bird? One, maybe two, more? Pecking and screeching, ducking into an upside-down hanging umbrella on the ceiling of the Dream House.

Sidney, Sidney, open the door, the door, let them out!

I vaguely see Sidney for a moment, not like Sidney but like a grainy shadow. He ups and turns towards the door, silent. He doesn't respond; only shifts in the darkness . . .

Sidney? Open the door. Can you open the door?

Why's he ignoring me? The birds are still screeching

Sidney says nothing. His silhouette is crouched over, cowering in the corner . . . his hands over his face. He looks little and young, far away from the cocky little kid hanging out over the fence. He turns to face me and that is when I notice . . . he looks like –

MY DAD!

He looks so much like my dad that I can't take it. My mouth fills with saliva and I tremble, feeling volts shooting through my arms and legs.

✦ *Sidney? The door . . .*

And he stares at me with my dad's face looming out of his skull, still saying nothing.

I lose my balance and half fall, half jump off the desk and onto the floor where I manage to kick the door. It waves open, flying off the hinges, stopping only as it thuds into the fence behind, battering open and closed like the wing of a bird. Then I leap up, whacking my arm against the hanging umbrella. Dust spirals out of the spokes and so do the birds, circling, before darting from the Dream House into the outside wind.

✦ *Sidney? Sidney?*

But he's not there.

Sidney has gone.

49.

I gather myself up as quick as I can. I haven't got any shoes on and I leg it back into the house and up into my room and into my bed, fully clothed. I am freezing cold, and I pull the covers over my head and shiver. I can't stop shivering. I wrap myself up tight in the blanket. The chills are so cold they are burning. My heart is pounding out of my chest. I turn to the side. I hold myself. Sweat begins to trickle from my face at such a speed. I am drenched.

I could be sick.

I am not ready. I am not ready. I don't want to see you, Dad. I'm too scared.

Make it stop. Make it stop.

The sheets over my head seem to suffocate me. My back sticks to the bed.

I close my eyes shut. Go away. Go away.

But the feeling doesn't go away because the feeling is me.

It's me.

50.

My head is broken.
My head is actually broken.
Who do I tell that my mind has broken?
If you break your leg, you go to hospital.
Where do I go? What do I do?
It's too much.

It hurts.
It's so painful.
I can't.

51.

Sparky knocks on my door.

➫ *Rex? Rex? Can I come in?*

He has a cup of tea for me.

➫ *Rex? Are you all right?*

> PLEASE DON'T LEAVE ME.
> DON'T LEAVE ME ALONE WITH
> MY THOUGHTS IN MY HEAD
> ON THIS NIGHTMARE CAROUSEL
> THAT I CAN'T GET OFF.

But I can't speak.

Beautiful day outside . . .

IT DOESN'T MATTER.

RIP YOURSELF OUT OF THE BED.

STAND UP. BE TALL.

RIP YOURSELF OUT OF THE BED, REX.

SIT UP. DRINK THE TEA.

SAY GOOD MORNING.

GET UP.

EAT BREAKFAST.
GO OUT. BE NORMAL.
REX. REX. REX.

OK, I'll just leave this here for you. I'll be downstairs if you need me.

And he closes the door gently behind him.

There was a blackout in the house but the lights are all on.

52.

I remember when I was ten years old. Dad wasn't well but he was in a good mood. We were hungry and he said we could have pizza for dinner.

For the first time he let me walk up to the top of the road to pick up pizza for us from the kebab shop – they had a proper wood-fired oven and their pizza was really good. I was so excited for the mission. I was going ALL BY MYSELF. I would NOT let Dad down. It was a summer's evening and I knew the road well. I smiled at the neighbours on my walk up. Clinging onto the money in my sweaty clamped palm.

They might be surprised to see a small child collecting pizza but I was ready for my entrance: 'Hey, this is just me. By the way I'm a legit adult now and I'm just picking up a few pizzas like a responsible member of the community, no big deal.'

I went into the takeaway shop and was waiting for our pizza. I had a long wait because the pizzas had only just gone into the oven and I was early because of my eagerness. A gang of boys walked in. They were wearing tracksuits and clown masks.

I remember my heart starting to beat fast. *Hurry up with the pizza.* I knew I shouldn't freak out but just stay calm. At first the boys started playing around and being stupid and annoying. I had seen boys like this in the area. I smiled politely and minded my own business.

They were winding the pizza guys up, fiddling with the posters on the wall and banging the sauces on the counter. Asking for free food. The pizza guys were doing a good job of remaining calm too. Keeping the mood tame. I didn't feel too scared because the shop seemed to have it under control. And it was sunny outside.

Nothing bad EVER happens when it's sunny. Does it?

I could see my school from the shop and my house was just a few minutes away. This reassured me.

But then the boys became rude and aggressive. The mood began to accelerate. They were being dominant and forward. Overexcited in their stupid masks and immunity. They had a sense of freedom. Of invincibility.

They were probably only about fourteen – a bit older than I am now – but in my head, at the time, they were fully grown giants. Their behaviour was a bit cartoon-like and larger than life. The alarm system of my body was alerting me that something wasn't right.

One of the pizza men took my hand and invited me to stand behind the counter with him as he argued with the boys and warned that he'd call the police if they didn't leave. I snuck behind the counter and watched, eyes peeping through the glass panel. The clown boys eventually left, bored, realising they weren't going to get any free food.

I peeped my head round the side of the counter to watch them leave the shop. Relieved to see them exit.

As they were walking away one of the boys bent down on his knees and looked me straight in the eyes. I saw his dark pupils flickering through the two cut-out eyeholes in his rubber mask, and he said one thing:

Laughed and then walked off.

I ran home with the pizza stacked, hot, on my forearms, sick gathering in my throat.

I couldn't eat a bite.

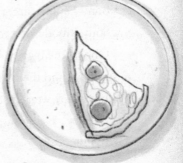

I didn't tell my dad about the clown boys because I wanted him to trust me and feel safe to let me do missions by myself in the future.

I didn't want him to feel bad. Or responsible. We knew his illness was getting worse and I didn't want him to think he was leaving me behind for the baddies of the world to devour me. And he'd be unable to protect me. Because he wouldn't be there.

I didn't want to make it about me. I didn't want him to worry.

I wanted him to think I'd be OK without him.

But the truth was – I wouldn't ever be OK without him.

I never wanted to collect the pizzas again. I was too scared.

In fact, I don't really even like pizza any more.

53.

Knock knock.

  Rex . . . Rex . . . it's me. It's Mum.

Lottie barges the door open without giving me a chance to reply.

She points at me and stomps right over.

  Hey, Lottie!

I smile. A real one.

I kiss her on her chubby hand.

  Why are you sleeping, Rex?

  I'm not asleep. I'm awake. Look, I'm talking to you.

  Why are you in bed?

  Because I'm tired.

  Why?

  Because I am.

  Why?

Mum gives Lottie her sticker book and comes to sit next to me. She strokes my hair. She says I look 'poorly'.

  I think it's time you came home with us.

  I don't want to.

I'm not ready. I don't exactly want to stay either, but I don't want to leave.

  Well, what do you want?

  I don't know what I want.

♪ *I'm sorry, Rexy. Well, here's an idea, let me help you by making a decision for you. I think it's time to come home, love, to see Dylan and Warren. Maddie's called a couple of times too. Have you not been replying to anyone's messages?*

✤ *I don't want to come back yet.*

♪ *It's not a good idea to run away.*

How can I tell her that I am trying to do the exact opposite of that?

✤ *Does Sparky want me to leave?*

♪ *What? No! Course not! Sparky never wants you to leave; he loves having you around. It's my idea . . .*

I want to cry hearing Mum say that. But I say nothing.

♪ *Some normality, bean? Think about school at some point? Sleep in your own bed?*

She pauses and comes towards me . . .

♪ *Bit of mummy cuddles?*

I shrug out of the cuddle and pick up Lottie. I do miss her. The gap between her teeth. She beeps my nose.

○ *Beep. Beep.*

She smiles.

I beep hers back.

✤ *Not yet, Mum. Soon but not yet.*

54.

TUG. TUG. TUG.

COME ALONG. COME ALONG . . .

I knew this meant I had to go back . . .

Not home . . . to the Dream House.

55.

This time I take the torch hanging by the back door.

Where is Sidney? It feels like I am somehow betraying him by not going back with him. Which is weird – it has nothing to do with him!

Maybe I scared him off? It was such an odd moment I –

But there he is. Waiting.

🐦 *Sidney?*

🐷 *Mate, where have you been?*

🐦 *Where have I been? You're the one that ran off!*

🐷 *Yeah, I had about nineteen crows in my hair, that's why. I could have got rabies.*

Coward.

🐷 *See that scratch there? That's from one of them crows.*

🐦 *I don't think they were crows. They were sparrows.*

🐷 *I don't know anything about birds, mate, but that was NO sparrow. It was like a vampire. You know in the films when loads of birds come together to make Dracula . . .? That was some madness in there.*

I begin making some space between the leaves and stalks and the door.

🐟 *Oi, you're not going back in, are you?*

✚ *Of course I am. I have to.*

🐟 *You don't have to do anything! Don't you know that? 'Oh, I have to do this. I have to do that.' The cool thing about life is that you actually don't. Just forget about it, move on!*

✚ *Some things you do have to do.*

🐟 *No, you don't. Ask me why I'm never at school. Because I simply don't want to go. That's why. My mum can't control me. Nobody can. But why fight against what I am? That's me.*

✚ *I'm going back in.*

🐟 *Into Draccie's dungeon. You're brave.*

✚ *Are you coming?*

🐟 *Absolutely not. No way.*

✚ *Well, I feel better that I've asked you.*

🐟 *I'm going back indoors, whacking the oven up to max and slinging in a whole pack of fish fingers. Hey, want me to bring you one out?*

✚ *No thanks.*

🐟 *I tell you what? I'll leave you one on the fence just in case.*

56.

When I hear Sidney's feet pounding back
towards the house. I face the Dream House.
Close my eyes. Take a breath and open up the door.

57.

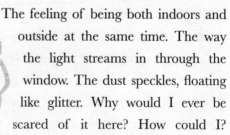

I hold the torch close to my chest as I creep inside,
feeling the weight of it in my hand. Are they meant
to double up as weapons to knock out burglars?

INSIDE

It is the same as it always was.
Preserved in time. The smell – I have
it now. I feel the walls. The shine of
the posters and the wilting cardboard
underneath, fluffy, almost wet with
dampness but not bad. The stillness. The muted silence.
The feeling of being both indoors and
outside at the same time. The way
the light streams in through the
window. The dust speckles, floating
like glitter. Why would I ever be
scared of it here? How could I?

It was my happy place.

It is mine. For being alive in. For dreaming inside of. For thinking of new ideas. To be alone, to keep me safe. I am glad Sidney refused to come in; it is my place, my secret. Maybe the Dream House even pushed him out intentionally?

I find my head filling with thoughts I had when I was young. Memories, songs from the radio, theme tunes from TV. Potato waffles and Neapolitan ice cream.

I sit at the desk. I feel the wood. I see my name engraved – Dad did that. I feel the grooves with my finger.

And then I let myself pull out the drawer.

There is an envelope . . .

REX

58.

Dear Rex,

If you are reading this, it means I am with Elvis now. Sorry about that. I had wanted to see you grow up. I had wanted to see if you'd end up with a beer belly like me. If you'd get a beard for a bit. What you'd like doing. What you'd end up doing. If you'd become a dad yourself. I often catch myself daydreaming of meeting your children. Isn't that strange? That you are my baby and then you'll maybe one day have babies yourself?

You'll always be my baby.

I hear his voice so loud in my head it's as though Dad's actually there. You know when you get tingles and shivers up your spine when somebody whispers in your ear?

I'm sure it was very difficult for you to come back here. Bet Sparky's doing your head in, isn't he? But he's a very good friend. The best. And I gave him this – to keep for you – because, it occurred to me, that you only knew me as Dad. You never knew me as Michael. (Although you heard your mum shout it at me 500 times a day!)

So, I wanted to take you back . . . and show you . . . who I was/am . . . depending on how you like to see a dead person.

Now, when you came to see me at the hospital . . . Horrible thing when you want to see your child and then don't at the same time because you don't want them to see you in any way that isn't great. And I know, I know, you don't have to tell me, I looked ABSOLUTELY FANTASTIC! I mean, talk about PRIME YEARS.

I feel myself laugh. The laughter turns into tears. Big globe tears that fall from my face and plop onto the words. I wipe them away quick as though somebody is watching. I want to put the letter down and have a break from it. It's too much. Then, at the same time, I can't wait to read every word . . . and then I never want it to end . . . I look out at the garden . . . I can almost see him walking towards me, waving . . . beer in hand . . . and I carry on . . .

Cancer has not been kind to my looks. I used to have muscle! I actually at one point even had a six-pack (if I breathed in really hard and tensed). I know right now, in your memory, I probably looked scary to you: old, pale, thin . . . grey. My legs are bloated. I am all crunched up in the bed. Hard to imagine me playing football on the common and chasing you in the woods, isn't it?

You would be the one lifting me now!

Maybe not? Maybe you see me at a better time?

Rex?

✢ *Dad?*

Why do I suddenly feel like he's . . .

He's here. No. Dad. Dad. Dad. No.

I don't want to see you, I'm too scared.

In the hospital gown. With the drip. And the old face.

No, please. I don't want to look.

I hide my eyes.

He's a light blue-and-white cloud, a shape in the corner of my eye, crouched down. Weak. Frail.

In the gaps between my fingers, I begin to read again.

You can't say I didn't have cheekbones! Just before I got unwell things were going the opposite – very well. I had scored pretty much the best goal of my whole life. Your mum and I had just had Lottie and she was beautiful. You were about to start at a good school and I had been promoted to head officer at the care unit. Even though we already knew I was that anyway and they'd just at last decided to pay me properly. We'd finally got enough money together to get the bathroom done and we'd booked France too.

We never made it there in the end, did we?

Plus, that fantastic new pub opened right by us with over thirty different delicious beers on tap.

About France, though. I am sorry about that. I would have loved to feel the sun on my skin. I would have loved to dunk your head under, to see your eyelashes pronged spiky with water drops. Watch your freckles appear. To eat French fries by the pool, a cold beer. You swimming, bringing your head up from underneath the chlorine. To be with you and Lottie in her silly little swimming costume and your mum, your beautiful mum. There was a moment when I actually thought I had it all.

No, I did. I did have it all.

I feel the weight of his hand on my shoulder. And I am so scared I want to cry but I don't want him to take it away. He's there. He's actually there. This can't be real. He's so close I can smell him. Newspapers . . . coffee . . . aftershave . . . mud . . .

His voice sounds lighter. Younger. Brighter.

I met your mum when I was twenty-two. She worked at a video store. Do you remember videos? Like giant tapes. Remember tapes? Her shop was called BLOCKBUSTER VIDEO and it would be a treat to go there and rent a film. Imagine a library but for films. Something to look forward to. You could get ice cream and popcorn there too. When it was time to return your film, you had to rewind it first and then drop it in this little postbox.

Anyway. I was always in there, on my own or with friends. I'd see your mum. She was pretty – always with different hair. Bleached or short or pink or red. Blue, I think, once. Once shaved.

We'd smile.

One time I went in to get my video and I had a girl with me. No biggie. Erin. It didn't work out, obviously.

Your mum looked livid. I won't lie. Then I got a call from Blockbuster Video. It was your mum.

Apparently I hadn't rewound *Venom* back (a terribly sexist film about an angry beekeeper). She was furious. She said, 'How would you like it if somebody didn't rewind a tape for you?'

We always joked about that. When your mum would go 'Venomous' on you.

Between you and me – I think I just annoyed her because of The Girl. Jealous!

I had an idea; I made a video for your mum, of me, asking her out. Only short. I made a little cover for the case too and addressed it to her . . . Well, 'For the Girl at Blockbuster who is always colouring her hair and telling off the customers . . .'

And I didn't bother winding it back either.

I see Dad; he looks young in a denim jacket covered in badges. A spiky haircut and boots.

I was all grown-up. It was time to leave Grandma Lou and Pops (Mum and Dad). Your mum and I got a flat in south London as your mum got a transfer to be a manager of a big new Blockbuster and so I left home . . .

You do know where I grew up, don't you? Right behind where you are sitting now.

My knees turn to jelly. I feel sick. My heart is in my mouth.

That was my house that backed onto Sparky's. That was how we met, over the fence, as kids. Sparky never left his family home!

I nearly throw up. Dad lived in – wait – that is Sidney's house . . .

And that desk you're sitting at, that was my desk – did you know that? One of those things you're always telling kids and they don't seem to listen to at the time. Did you see the name 'Julie' scratched into the side? Don't show your mum – she was my first girlfriend!

JULIE

♣ *YES, DAD, YOU ALWAYS TOLD ME!*

Like something from the olden days, isn't it? I never liked school, best thing that's come out of it for me was that desk.

Rex. Sparky has lots of photos to show you, of me and your mum and Sparky and you lot as kids. Please look at them. Even if not for yourself – keep an old boy happy!

Oh God, kid. I love you.

I know you were getting into a grunge phase – that still happening or have you grown out of that?

People used to say you were sensitive, in tune with the world – I used to have a go at Sparky for that, but I was probably envious of how much life seemed to touch him. Sensitivity is actually a superpower. Never lose that. I have never been prouder of anybody in my life than I am of you. You are the greatest thing about me.

Please don't remember me how I was in the hospital. Remember me as YOU. Because I was you once. Young, free, a child. Electric energy rushing through my veins with so much to do.

I am always with you. If you ever need reminding, just look in the mirror. You'll see I am always in you.

I left you behind to remind you of me.

I am just here.

I am here.

There is just so much to do.

I love you for ever.

Just look up and . . .

I see Sparky leaning against the garden door, wide open with the sunshine pouring in. Arms folded with a steaming hot mug in his hand. Tears streaming down his face as always.

And I smile and wave.

He nods in pride.

And I catch my reflection in the window.

DAD.

Do you see me now?

59.

I fall onto the desk.
I've never cried so hard. I cry
until the desk feels like it has been
washed out to sea, as if the Dream
House has been miraculously flooded.
I lose it all. I give myself up. I hand myself
over. The garden, a monsoon, sunk under the
depth of my grief. I miss you so much. It's too
much. It's too heavy to carry, Dad. It's too
heavy to carry on my own.

*You don't have to. You don't have to do
anything at all.*

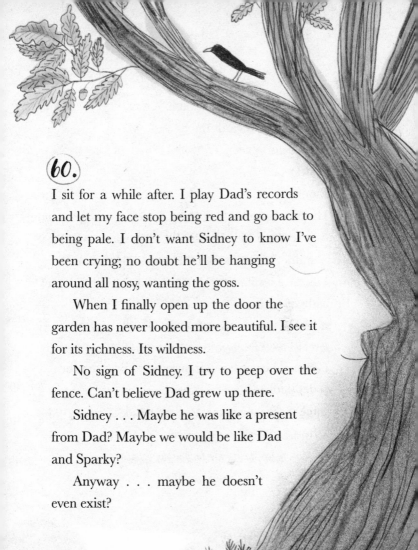

60.

I sit for a while after. I play Dad's records
and let my face stop being red and go back to
being pale. I don't want Sidney to know I've
been crying; no doubt he'll be hanging
around all nosy, wanting the goss.

When I finally open up the door the
garden has never looked more beautiful. I see it
for its richness. Its wildness.

No sign of Sidney. I try to peep over the
fence. Can't believe Dad grew up there.

Sidney . . . Maybe he was like a present
from Dad? Maybe we would be like Dad
and Sparky?

Anyway . . . maybe he doesn't
even exist?

61.

I'm starving. I could eat a house. A city.

I head back towards the house.

I can hear talking.

Sparky and . . .

Sidney.

He looks up at me with a new face now, an expression I've not seen on him before, one that wipes away that usual smirk. It's the look of kindness. He's borrowing my loss, he's feeling it with me, he's carrying my grief. Empathy.

Knew there was something going on with you, Rex. Sparky just told me. Sorry about your dad.

I clench my jaw.

Thanks.

I feel a weight off my chest. Sidney pulls something out of his pocket.

See? Told you I'd save you a fish finger.